BEASTS
—OF—
OLYMPUS

For Nikki Robinson-Smith—with thanks for everything—LC
For Finnegan, who reminds me to play—BB

GROSSET & DUNLAP
Penguin Young Readers Group
An Imprint of Penguin Random House LLC

The publisher does not have any control over and does not assume any responsibility
for author or third-party websites or their content.

Text copyright © 2017 by Lucy Coats. Illustrations copyright © 2017 by Brett Bean. All rights reserved.
Published by Grosset & Dunlap, an imprint of Penguin Random House LLC, 345 Hudson Street, New York,
New York 10014. GROSSET & DUNLAP is a trademark of Penguin Random House LLC.
Printed in the USA.

Library of Congress Cataloging-in-Publication Data is available.

ISBN 9780451534330   10 9 8 7 6 5 4 3 2 1

BEASTS
—OF—
OLYMPUS

by Lucy Coats   art by Brett Bean

Gods of the North

GROSSET & DUNLAP
An Imprint of Penguin Random House

CHAPTER 1

STRANGER!

Demon secretly breathed out a sigh of relief as he waved farewell to his teacher. The centaur headed off down the steep slope of Mount Pelion. Chiron carried a large bundle in his arms that was cooing and gurgling. Baby Hygeia was all cured now, so he was taking her home to her parents at last. Demon could finally get on with a full day of quiet studying. Babysitting, he decided, was a very tiring job. He much preferred looking after his beasts.

However, Chiron liked him to write up his

notes on each case. First of all, Demon put on his pink-tinted opticles and got out the beautiful red-and-gold leather journal that the goddess Athena had given him for saving the phoenix. He sucked on the end of his quill for a moment and then began to form careful letters on the page as the pink light of dawn lit up the cave.

Babies: How to Look After Them, he wrote. But before he could get down another word, there was a whooshing sound outside the cave. A wisp of multicolored light snaked in and tapped him on the shoulder.

"That faun Bion is in trouble again," said Iris, goddess of the rainbow. "Hop in. You're needed back at the Stables."

This time, Demon's sigh was loud and impatient. It was taking much longer than he'd expected to teach his brand-new assistant all the stuff he needed to know about the Stables of the Gods.

With Demon needing to explain everything about a hundred times, it was all taking twice as long as it should have.

"What's he gone and done now?" he asked rather wearily as he climbed aboard. He wasn't sure he was cut out for being a teacher.

"I believe the griffin mentioned something about a bull fight and a pen on fire." Demon closed his eyes and clenched his jaw. This was the third incident in as many days. The two brass bulls were becoming a pain in his neck.

"You'd better hurry, Iris," he said.

"Hold on to your hair, then," said the rainbow goddess as she whisked him up and away to Olympus.

Demon pulled a neatly folded packet out of one of the rather messy drawers in the hospital shed and pointed to it with a stern finger.

"This," he said, waving it under the faun's nose, "is the Patent Pyro-Protection Suit. Remember? The one you have to put on to keep yourself safe when the fiery beasts get going. How many times have I told you that?"

Bion hung his head. Half the curly hair on his head was singed and smoking slightly, and one arm was red and burnt-looking.

"Sorry, Demon," he mumbled. "I forgot. Khalko and Kafto started fighting again, and then they got out and set the sun hay on fire, and I just panicked a bit. Some of it's all burnt and wet now. Doris was rather enthusiastic with the water buckets."

"Right," Demon said. "I'm fed up with those two bully boys. If they won't stop fighting and flaming, we'll have to separate them. Come on, you can help." He looked at Bion. "But first we'd better put some soothing ointment on those burns. I think I've got some left from when I treated the big winged horse."

Just as they were persuading a reluctant Khalko to enter his new fireproof pen, there was an unusual uproar outside.

"Hey, Pan's scrawny kid," said a familiar voice. "Come quick—something's happening!" It was the griffin—and its orange eyes were blazing with excitement. Demon latched the pen firmly, and then ran out with Bion.

Something was indeed happening. A chattering commotion came from a group of nymphs and cherubs hovering around a stranger who was clad in a long cloak of white furs and carrying a golden horn that twisted around his whole body like a giant snake. His hair was also white, and his white beard was plaited into three jutting forks. As Demon came closer, he saw that the man's eyes were the pale white-blue of an early winter sky.

"Who in the world is that?" he whispered to the griffin.

"Dunno," it said.
"Never seen him
before."

The stranger put the horn to his lips and blew. It made a sound like no other Demon had ever heard, and suddenly his skin prickled as if he'd been dipped in deep black water on the coldest-ever winter day. Then the stranger began to shout, and his voice filled the whole of Olympus.

"Hear me, hear me, O mighty Zeus. I am Heimdall, herald of Asgard, and I am sent to bring you news from the North." As he spoke, there was a crash of thunder, and Zeus appeared, with Hera beside him. As lightning flashed around them, and the sky darkened, the nymphs and cherubs all scattered, and Demon shrank back behind a nearby olive tree. The griffin and Bion skulked in behind him.

"And what news is that, O herald of Asgard?" Zeus said, his voice booming just as loudly.

"Why, the best of news," said Heimdall, baring his golden teeth in a grin like a shark Demon had once seen down in Poseidon's realm. "The gods of the North are coming to visit you. It's party time! See ya later, Thunder Maker!" And then he disappeared in a blast of icy white light, leaving behind a large scroll fluttering through the air, and a huge pile of what looked like man-size stone jars.

"Well," said Hera, snatching the scroll and peering at it before thrusting it at Zeus. "I call that very rude. Inviting themselves to stay like that. Who do these Northern gods think they are?" She swept off, back to her palace, muttering, and Demon shrank even farther behind the tree, hoping she wouldn't see him. The queen of the gods wasn't exactly known for her sunny temper, and he didn't fancy being frazzled to a frizzle before he'd even seen what these new gods looked like.

Zeus frowned as he read the scroll, and as he stalked forward to examine the stone jars, a low mutter of thunder growled overhead. Picking one up as if it were a feather, he wrenched off the top with a *pop* and then looked inside, sniffing deeply as a cloud of foam spilled over the rim. Then he swung the jar up to his mouth and took a cautious swig of whatever was inside. All at once, a change came over his face. He took a great gulp, then another, and another.

"Ahhh," he sighed, wiping foam off his beard and setting down the empty jar and picking up another. "Mead! Delicious. Almost better than Dionysus's grape brew." Straightening up to his full height, his eyes swept around Olympus, finally settling on Demon, who automatically began to quake with fear. But whatever Zeus had drunk seemed to have put him in a good mood.

"Ah, Pandemonius," he said. "I want every last inhabitant of Olympus outside my palace before Helios and his chariot have reached the midpoint of the sky. Run around and tell them all, would you?"

"Y-yes, Your Mighty Thunderousness," Demon said, dropping to his knees. Then a thought hit him. "Er, do you mean I'm to tell the other gods and goddesses, too?" he asked cautiously.

Zeus laughed. "Hera will have let most of them know already, but you'd better pop up to Hephaestus's forge. He never hears anything if he's banging about with those great hammers of his. Hurry up now, young Stable Master. There's no time to lose." With that he picked up yet another of the enormous stone jars and set off after Hera, humming a tune that sounded like stars grinding against each other.

Demon looked up at the sky. Helios's chariot didn't have much farther to go before the sun would be right overhead. Panic was starting to sink in when the griffin poked him in the back with its sharp beak.

"I'll let the nymphs and dryads know, Pan's

scrawny kid," it said. "And they'll tell the cherubs."

"And I'll tell the fauns from the kitchen," said Bion rather squeakily. An encounter with Zeus tended to make almost anyone a bit squeaky, Demon had found.

Thanking them over his shoulder, Demon ran as fast as he could up the mountain to find his old friend the blacksmith god, Hephaestus. Taking a quick look to make sure the dragon-mode danger sign wasn't anywhere in sight, he leaped over the Colchian Dragon's purple tail and ran into the dark, sooty cave. He followed the ringing sound of hammer on anvil to its source. Hephaestus had a grimy rag wrapped around his sweaty forehead, and he was battering away at a long sword that glowed cherry red from the heat of the fire. Demon jumped up and down to get the smith god's attention, and after one last mighty blow, Hephaestus plunged the sword into a nearby water trough, causing an explosion of hissing and steam.

"What?" he said, scowling. "I'm busy. Ares needs this sword by tonight. He's got another wretched war to fight."

"Never mind that," said Demon, panting and wheezing. "Zeus wants everyone outside the palace right now. He sent me to fetch you."

Muttering, the smith god put down his hammer. "Don't eat all the charcoal while I'm gone," he said to the dragon. But it took no notice, snoring quietly in the corner on a pile of golden armlets.

"Now, what's going on, young Pandemonius?" he asked. "And since when have you been my father's messenger?"

Panting even harder and running to keep up with the god's long strides, Demon explained. And as they got nearer to Zeus and Hera's palace, the sound of a great crowd rose to greet them.

"Scoot over, Pan's scrawny kid," said the griffin, joining them as Demon and Hephaestus squeezed past a chattering gaggle of fauns, Bion among them. "I'm not missing this."

And then, with a golden flash, Zeus was on the balcony above them with Hera and all the other gods and goddesses crowded in behind him. He held up a hand, and immediately there was silence.

"Odin and the gods of Asgard arrive in seven days," he said. "I want every flower polished, every palace painted. Olympus must be perfect. We will not be shamed before the gods of the North, will we?"

"NO!" came the reply, so loud that Olympus shook with the force of it.

CHAPTER 2

WINGS ON FIRE

"You've got some tidying up to do, Pan's scrawny kid," said the griffin, reaching out a claw and patting some mucky straw blowing about. Demon looked around. It was true. The Stables weren't as immaculate as he would have liked. There were cobwebs in some of the corners, and Doris the Hydra had dropped a messy trail of ambrosia crumbs on the floor. He sniffed. There was also a distinct smell of burnt hay, mixed with a bit of a pooey stench.

"Come on, Bion," he said. "Let's find the buckets." But Bion was staring at something over Demon's shoulder. All at once, the faun gasped and fell flat on his face.

Demon whipped around.

Zeus was standing right there, leaning against the huge door frame. Demon's knees began to tremble. This was definitely not the happy Zeus of earlier that day. He was rubbing his temples as if he had a headache.

The king of the gods scowled, and Demon braced himself. Was this it? Was Zeus going to zap him into charcoal at last? He squeezed his eyes shut and hunched his shoulders tightly around his ears, waiting.

"PANDEMONIUS!" The great booming voice rang out, making Demon's eyes pop open despite his fear. His mouth was as dry as an empty well, but he forced himself to speak.

"Y-yes, Your Tremendous Thunderousness. H-how can I help you?"

Zeus bent down and picked up Demon with one thumb and finger, so that he was dangling just in front of Zeus's nose.

"Listen well, young Stable Master! You will perform with some of your flying horses as part of the entertainment after the feast. Make it magnificent, make it memorable. I leave it to you, boy."

He cast his piercing blue eyes over the Stables, wrinkling his nose. "Get rid of the smell, too. I want this place and every beast in it polished to perfection. I shall be giving our guests the grand tour of Olympus."

Demon didn't dare move, terrified that Zeus was going to drop him. The god glared at him.

"DO I MAKE MYSELF CLEAR?" he barked. Demon found himself nodding so hard, he thought his head was going to drop off.

"Yes, Your Superb Scariness," he whispered. "I understand."

Without quite knowing how, he found himself on the ground again, all in a heap. Zeus was nowhere to be seen, Bion was sobbing in a corner, and even the griffin had its wings over its eyes.

Demon's mind was racing. An aerial display with the winged horses. He could do that, and maybe he could get the boss horse, Keith, to—

His mind ground to a halt suddenly, remembering, and his stomach dropped like a stone.

Of course!

All the winged horses were down on earth. Iris had refused to carry them ever again after they pooed all over her. He had no way of getting them back up to Olympus.

"Oh no," he groaned. "What am I going to do?"

"Do about what?" asked the griffin.

Demon explained.

"Sounds like you're in trouble again, Pan's scrawny kid," it said, yawning. "I'm off for a nap. Gods make my beak ache. And if you think you're roping me into this aerial performance thingy, then think again." With that, it stalked off and lay down in its pen, all four paws in the air.

"I've got an idea," said Bion timidly. "If Iris won't do it, what about Golden Dog? Couldn't he bring back the horses?"

Demon nearly hugged him. Golden Dog had the strange ability of slipping through the cracks in time and space, and he could take people along with him.

"Brilliant!" he said. "Well done, Bion. Let's go and find him right now."

Bion blushed with pleasure.

Unfortunately, Golden Dog was not in his usual place, curled up with the magic nanny goat, Amaltheia.

"Mehhh!" she bleated as Demon entered her luxurious pen. "Was that my little Zeusie I heard shouting? Why didn't he come and see me?"

"I think he was a bit busy," Demon said. "I'm

sure he'll be in to see you soon. Now, do you know where Golden is?"

"He left this morning," Amaltheia said. "I don't know where he went. He never tells me anything, silly hound."

"Can you call him back?" Demon pleaded. "It's really urgent." The old goat butted him in the leg.

"I'll try," she said. "Because it's you, young Pandemonius. But mind you get one of those nice nymphs to come and comb out my curls for me." She closed her eyes and let out three high, clear bleats, then three very low ones. Almost at once, there was a distant bark, sounding as if it were coming from the end of a very long tunnel, and then, in a frantic flurry of legs, waving tail, and tiny golden stars, the dog appeared out of nowhere.

Once all the usual ritual of bouncing and jumping up and snuffly licking of faces was done, Demon explained what he needed.

"Ooh! Fun!" Golden Dog barked. "Grab my ears, then, Demon! Let's go!"

Demon had done this before, but the dizzy, whooshing sensation still made his stomach feel as if it were falling out of his feet. Within less than a breath, though, he was stumbling onto the sunny slope where the winged horses liked to graze. As he and Golden Dog appeared out of nowhere, the herd whinnied in alarm and took off into the air.

"It's all right," Demon called to them. "It's only me!" Slowly the little horses settled to earth again, and Keith, the boss horse, trotted up to him, his daughter, Sky Pearl, behind him.

"Oh!" said Demon. "When did you get back?" He'd left Sky Pearl with his friend Prince Peleus in the Mountains of Burning Sand after their adventure with the phoenix.

"Today-hey-hey," she whinnied. "I dropped Peleus off at his dad's palace. They gave me minty sweeties." She nuzzled his tunic. "I LIKE minty sweeties!"

"I'll make you some," Demon promised. "But now you all have to come back to Olympus with Golden Dog and me. Zeus needs us. Get into a line and hold on to one another's tails!"

He turned to Golden Dog, keeping his fingers crossed that the idea would work.

"We'd better do this in twos and threes."

By the time all the little horses had finally staggered into their paddock, looking a bit stunned by the short journey, Helios had nearly driven his sun chariot over the horizon. Demon and Bion brought them a big barrowful of unburnt sun hay.

"You can rest tonight," Demon said. "But first thing tomorrow, we have a performance to plan!"

Demon lay awake under his spider-silk blanket. He and Bion had started in on scrubbing every inch of the Stables before they went to bed. His body was exhausted, but his mind refused to shut down. *Magnificent* and *memorable* was what Zeus had demanded. But how was he going to make sure his aerial display was both?

"Maybe gold paint," he muttered. "Or streamers . . ."

"Whaa . . . ?" murmured Bion sleepily from the next-door pallet.

"Never mind," Demon whispered. Eventually, he dozed off, but his dreams were full of wings and fire.

The next morning, he set Bion to boiling up a small pot of peppermint leaves and honey for Sky Pearl's sweeties, and a much huger pot of eucalyptus leaves, lemons, and pine needles.

"We have to make the poo chute smell nice," he

said. "This should do it." He wasn't sure that the hundred-armed monsters at the bottom of the poo chute were going to appreciate the nice smell much, but they'd just have to put up with it.

When he arrived at the paddock, the winged horses were in an excited huddle of wings and hooves.

"Look, De-he-he-mon!" Keith whinnied. Whirling around, he and Sky Pearl set off at a canter, one swerving left and the other right, with half the herd following each of them. They soared into the air and began a complicated series of loop-the-loops and spirals high in the sky. Then they came together behind Keith in a big *V* and swooped down low over Demon's head, so that he was nearly knocked over by the breeze of their wings.

He clapped.

"Amazing!" he yelled. But it was still not quite marvelous or memorable enough. How could he make the display good enough that Zeus wouldn't spike him with a lightning bolt? Suddenly he remembered his dreams of the night before. Wings . . . and fire.

"Keep practicing!" he called. "I've got an idea." And he started to run up the mountain toward Hephaestus's forge.

The forge was buzzing with activity. Golden automatons were running about everywhere, and the place was full of heat and sparkle. Piles of purple and orange fire-jewels lay everywhere, along with rubies and pearls and all manner of other gemstones. Hephaestus hunched over a delicate piece of jewelry, alternately teasing out strands of gold with a tiny pair of tongs and tapping them with a small silver hammer.

"Can I borrow the Colchian Dragon, please?" Demon shouted.

"Take him with pleasure!" Hephaestus said, not looking up. "We're all tripping over him. You'd be doing me a favor. I've got to make enough jewelry for all the goddesses, as well as gifts for all our visitors." He wiped a sweaty hand over his forehead and started tapping again.

"What do you need me for?" asked the dragon, snatching up a last mouthful of charcoal. His bright purple tail made a slithery sound on the rocks.

"You'll see," said Demon. He crossed his fingers as he spoke, though, because there was a big danger that it could all go horribly wrong.

CHAPTER 3

THE SHIP OF CLOUDS

"Like this, but a lot bigger." Demon sketched a large circle in the air with his hand. "Do you think you can do it?"

The Colchian Dragon blinked lazily and let out a tiny charcoaly belch.

"What happens if I get scared and, you know . . ." It nodded toward its back end. When Demon had first met it, it had been the fartiest creature ever, and had nearly blown Olympus to smithereens.

"You won't," said Demon firmly. "And anyway, I

thought the charcoal-and-peppermint diet fixed all that."

"Oh, well," said the dragon. "I'll give it a go." It drew in a deep breath and turned its muzzle to the sky. Then, very gently, it puffed out. With a little *pop*, a perfect ring of fire floated into the air, widening as it went, then another and another.

Demon punched a fist into the air. "YES! Now, Keith, let's see if you and the herd can fly through the rings."

A few days (and a couple of nearly singed wingtips) later, the dragon and Keith's team of fliers had put together a display that even Demon thought was magnificent and marvelous enough for the gods. He'd persuaded one of the nymphs to make some flower-petal-and-silver-ribbon streamers for him, and he and Bion were going to braid them into all the horses' manes and tails just before the performance. Zeus had sent over the running order—the winged horses were to close the show, and he'd also sent over strict instructions about what they were to do at the very end. Demon just hoped it would work.

Meanwhile, all the beasts in the Stables had been shampooed and polished and brushed till they shone, though the giant scorpion had objected rather violently and tried to sting Doris the Hydra to death. Not a speck of dust or dirt remained. Every instrument in the hospital shed gleamed, and every bandage was snowy white. Even the poo chute sparkled, though the hundred-armed monsters were not at all happy with their new poo-plus-eucalyptus-drain-cleanser diet.

Demon looked around.

"I think we're ready," he said to Bion and the griffin. As he spoke, a large fluffy white cloud sailed across the sky.

"Oh no," said Bion. "I hope it isn't going to rain."

"That's no rain cloud, Faun Boy," said the griffin. "Look!" It pointed with a claw.

Demon's mouth fell open in a silent O of wonder, and he began to run. It seemed that all the other inhabitants of Olympus had the same idea, and soon a large chattering crowd had gathered.

Under the cloud, a huge sailing ship was gliding down toward Olympus, long and sleek, with round shields lining its sides. In a series of rainbow flashes, all the Olympian gods appeared, just as the ship slid gracefully to a halt.

It brought with it an icy breeze filled with the scent of cold, wild places—and also a slight smell of goat. A golden gangplank slid out of the side, and a tall, fierce-looking god strode down it, his long hair and beard floating around his face like tangled white thistledown. He wore a wide-brimmed hat and had a leather patch over his right eye. On each of his shoulders perched an enormous black raven. Beside him was an equally tall, snow-pale goddess wearing a crown of diamond icicles.

Behind them came a huge golden-haired god carrying a gigantic silver hammer, and then nine other gods and goddesses, including a tall, shifty-eyed figure right at the back, with a pointy beard and a silver helmet with large ram's horns attached to it. Demon couldn't see him very well. The figure seemed to slip in and out of view, blurring and changing shape, so that suddenly he was a proud mare, then a leaping salmon, and then a tiny bright green fly that buzzed off out of sight.

As soon as they had disembarked, the raven god turned to the cloud ship and snapped his fingers. All at once, the ship began to fold itself up, smaller and smaller until it lay at his feet, no bigger than a handkerchief. Demon's mouth dropped open as the god picked it up and put it in a pocket, but there was no time to wonder.

As Zeus and Hera stepped forward to greet the gods of the North, Apollo struck a chord on his silver lyre, and roses rained down out of the sky, making a sweet-smelling path before them.

"Greetings, Odin and all you gods of Asgard," Zeus boomed, and out of nowhere he produced a huge golden cup brimming with Dionysus's special red party drink. "Let us drink to friendship and harmony, then let us feast."

From among the crowd of nymphs, fauns, cherubs, and other beings, Demon watched anxiously. What if the Asgardians didn't like Dionysus's brew? What if they spat it out and then there was a war between the gods? The whole world might be frazzled to a frizzle. But all scary thoughts went right out of his head when Odin took the cup and drained it in one gulp.

"Good stuff," he said, clapping Zeus familiarly on the back. "Now, where's that feast you mentioned,

Thunder Maker? I'm starving."

It was the most magnificent spread Demon had ever seen, with laden tables scattered all around the beautiful garden that lay outside the palaces of the gods. Hestia and her kitchen helpers had outdone themselves, especially in the dessert department. Demon, however, was too nervous about the forthcoming performance to do more than nibble on a couple of his favorite honey cakes.

The gods were seated at the high table, a marvelous creation of snowy marble inlaid with ebony and gold olive branches. Every god and goddess had a different-looking chair, each covered with living symbols. Hera's was covered in blinking peacock-feather eyes, and Zeus's sizzled with tiny lightning bolts. Demon noticed that Odin's was covered with soaring ravens, but the two birds that had arrived with him were nowhere to be seen. He wondered for a moment where they'd gone, but just then the toasts started. It was nearly time.

"Come on, Bion," he whispered.

They both crept away from the feast and ran to the Stables. Keith, Sky Pearl, and the rest were in a high state of excitement as the sparkling flower streamers were attached.

"You look magnificent," said Demon. "Now, where's that dragon? Is he in position?" Running outside, he checked on the mountainside. Yes, there was a splash of purple above, and above that, high in the blue sky, two black dots circled.

Demon frowned. Were those Odin's ravens? He hoped they wouldn't get in the way.

"Come on," he said. "Time to go. Wait for Zeus's sky signal—and remember, no pooing on anyone's head!"

Heart beating faster than a running deer's, he went back to the feast. Catching Zeus's eye, he nodded. The horses were ready.

"We have a little surprise to welcome you, our honored godly guests," the king of the Olympian gods boomed. "So sit back and enjoy the show." With that, Hermes lifted a golden trumpet to his lips and blew one high note. First the nymphs danced, then the dryads performed a ballet with their trees, which twined about them like living partners. Hades had brought his skeleton guard with him, and they had a mock battle with some of Ares's soldiers, which ended with rather too many severed bony limbs for Demon's liking. Hades had also brought Demon's friend Orpheus with him. The misty musician played his ghostly lyre so beautifully that it made everyone weep. Flocks of kingfishers zipped through the air like tiny blue jewels. The tears were soon turned to laughter, though, when the cherubs and fauns did a funny little skit, imitating all the Olympians. Demon didn't know how they dared. Then Zeus held up his hand for silence.

"And now for our grand finale," he said. With that, he took a lightning bolt from his eagle, twirled it, and flung it upward, where it burst, turning the sky to incandescent whiteness.

The little winged horses took to the air in pairs, forming a huge circle above the feasting gods. Then they went into their routine. They flew so fast that the streamers looked like living rainbows, weaving patterns of loops and curls that looked like intricate writing across the white sky. Then the fire hoops appeared in the air, and the gods and goddesses whooped and cheered as the horses flew through and in and out of them. The final hoop floated down toward the feast, getting bigger and bigger, straightening out into a rope of fire.

Demon crossed his fingers and toes and everything else crossable. If this last bit didn't work . . .

The horses formed into pairs again, and with one last loop-the-loop, Sky Pearl and Keith arrowed low toward the fire rope, which they grabbed in their mouths. Flying even lower over the high table, they dropped the fire rope right over the gods and goddesses, where it burst in a shower of popping golden stars. And when the stars had cleared, each goddess was wearing a fabulous bracelet of sparkling jewels, and each god a spectacular armband.

"Magnificent!" shouted Odin, banging on the table with one enormous fist as the horses soared away back to the Stables. "The best yet!" And all the other Asgardians and Olympians agreed.

After receiving a congratulatory clap on the back from his dad, Pan, and an approving nod from Zeus, Demon headed up to Hephaestus's forge to thank the Colchian Dragon for his help. He then went back to the Stables to make sure Keith and his herd had extra ambrosia and hay, and to give them big pats. Later, after one last inspection of the Stables, he crept into bed and, snuggling down under his spider-silk blanket, he drifted off to the sound of Bion's little whiffling snores. As he slid into sleep, a shiny black feather floated down from the rafters above, and two shadows swooped down over him. But Demon was too tired to notice.

CHAPTER 4
AN UNEXPECTED JOURNEY

"Incoming," hissed the griffin, peering outside. "Incoming gods."

Demon and Bion had been up since before Eos threw back her pink dawn curtains, giving everything and everyone a final polish.

"Right, everyone," Demon said to all the beasts. "Best behavior, all of you. And, Doris, remember not to drool on the visitors." With that, he and Bion ran to the doors and flung them wide open, standing at attention with the griffin between them.

It had somehow persuaded Hephaestus to make it a golden collar and claw shields, and was wearing them proudly.

Zeus was striding toward them, with Odin beside him, ravens on his shoulders, and two other Asgardians trailing behind.

"Blimey, Pan's scrawny kid," said the griffin out of the side of its beak. "It's the two big chiefs and the pretty ones. Better watch your manners."

Demon was watching his manners so hard that his knees wobbled. He didn't even slap at the annoying bright green fly that was buzzing around his ear, for fear of being misunderstood.

"Well, Stable Master?" said the king of the Olympian gods. "Are you ready for us?"

"Yes, Your Thundery Tremendousness, we are," he said, bowing low. The griffin beside him tried to execute a sort of curtsy but got tangled in its own legs and fell over. Embarrassed, it sat down and began to preen its wing feathers.

"Sorry about that, Your Marvelousnesses," Demon said, blushing. It was not a good start. "Come right this way." But then he stopped. Odin was holding up a hand. Tiny snowflakes fell from his fingers, melting as they hit the ground.

"Just one moment, Thunder Maker." Suddenly his one green eye seemed to pierce Demon's skin, sucking out all his secrets, and then his ravens took off, gliding toward Demon on silent wings. As they swooped down, they plucked a tuft of hair from each side of his head, then soared off back to their master. Landing on his shoulders again, they cawed quietly into his ears. Demon began to shake like a leaf in a high wind. Had he done something wrong?

Was this the beginning of being slowly torn to death by raven pecks? But then Zeus was speaking.

"Is something the matter with my Stable Master, One-Eye?" he said, a slight edge to his voice.

Odin slung an arm over Zeus's shoulder. "Not a thing, old boy," he said. "In fact, he's the reason we're really here. We need to borrow him."

If Demon's mouth had fallen open any farther, it would have hit his toes.

"M-m-me, Your Serene Snowiness?" he stammered. "But why?"

"Yes, why do you need MY Stable Master?" said Zeus, his bushy eyebrows giving off little sparks of lightning. "Don't you have one of your own?"

"Well, we've got a little problem we hope he can fix," Odin said. "But I'll let the twins explain."

A god and a goddess stepped forward. They were both so incredibly golden that Demon could hardly look at them without being dazzled.

"I am Freya. What is your name, young Stable Master?" the goddess asked. She wore a cloak of shining bronze falcon feathers, and her voice was as soft as a summer breeze.

"P-Pandemonius," he stuttered. "Your Gorgeous Goldenosity." Freya smiled, and her teeth were as white as pearls. Demon tried hard not to fall over.

"Oh, I LIKE him, Frey!" she said to her brother. "None of you ever call me nice names."

"Never mind that," said the equally beautiful god. "Pandemonius, is it true that you've had some success in healing incurable immortal beasts?"

Demon blushed. "Well, I s-suppose so," he said modestly. "Kind of. I, er . . . I haven't had many failures so far."

"How about pigs?"

"N-no," Demon said slowly. "I haven't dealt with one of those yet."

"Here's the thing," said Frey. "My old boar,

Goldbristle, is losing his light. I drive along in the sky, and he just gets dimmer and dimmer."

"He's simply not shining properly anymore," said Freya. "Everything's all dark and horrid now in Asgard. And that means the plants are dying. None of the new crops I've planted have grown at all, and poor Idunn's apple trees are positively drooping."

"The long and short of it," Odin interrupted, "is that your friend Pegasus was talking to my horse, Sleipnir, and telling him how you'd helped heal his wounds. So I sent my ravens, Thought and Memory, to check up on you, and it seems you've got quite the reputation among the creatures of the world. The phoenix was particularly complimentary, they tell me. So there it is. Will you come back to Asgard with us and see if you can find out what's wrong with Goldbristle? None of our healers have a clue what's up with the old chap."

He cleared his throat and turned to Zeus.

"That's if you don't mind, of course, Thunder Maker," he said, narrowing that one green eye.

Zeus stroked his beard thoughtfully. "That depends," he said, "on the state in which we find these Stables, and the beasts within. I wouldn't want to lend you a Stable Master whose charges weren't up to snuff."

With that, he strode past Demon, whose heart had just somersaulted into his throat and was doing a little fear dance on his tonsils. He shuddered, and followed the four gods in, trailed by a nervous-looking Bion. *I might as well know the worst right away*, he thought, as the griffin disappeared. He didn't blame it.

Zeus and his companions poked into everything. Luckily, all the beasts behaved, though Amaltheia did try to scold Zeus for not visiting her, and the little winged horses were given special ear scratches and praise.

"What are those scars?" Freya asked, pointing to Doris's nine necks.

The old anger rose up in Demon's chest, driving out any fear. "Poor Hydra," he said, stroking the green head that was lovingly draped over his shoulder. "Horrible Heracles chopped off all its heads, so I had to stick them back on. I couldn't get rid of the scars, though." He kept his fingers crossed, praying that none of the gods would ask how he'd done it. He still wasn't sure that using one of Hera's magic golden apples had been entirely legal—and there was the worry that the tiny drip of juice that he had licked off his finger had made him a bit more immortal than he should be. Nobody knew about that—and Demon wanted to keep it that way.

"Impressive," said Odin, and Demon glowed. He didn't often get praise from a god.

Then Zeus made him show them everything in the hospital shed.

"What's that?" Frey asked, pointing to the silver box that stood, shiny and polished, in the center of the operating table.

"This is the magic medicine box Hephaestus made me, Your Gloriousness. Say hello, box," Demon said, tapping it. The magic medicine box let out a sudden stream of sparks and started to glow blue, making Frey jump a little.

"Exiting standby mode," it said. "Please wait." A tiny rainbow circle began to spin in its lid, then went out.

"State nature of medical problem," it said in its usual tinny voice. Demon sighed.

"Just greet the gods nicely, please," he said, trying not to sound cross.

The box emitted a rude raspberry sound. Demon went bright red.

"I'm so sorry, Your Magnificent Majesties," he said. "I think it might have picked up another bug.

I'll take it back to Hephaestus." Grabbing a linen cloth, he threw it over the box, hiding it. He knew perfectly well it didn't really have a bug. It was just being its usual grumpy self.

"We've seen enough," said Zeus. "If you can promise me that your assistant is capable of handling things in your absence, Pandemonius, then I think you may go to Asgard. I am very pleased with you, indeed."

"Th-thank you, Your Tremendous Thunderiness," he said, dropping to his knees as Zeus stretched down a hand to pat the top of his head.

"I think I'd better give you the gift of the tongues of men and gods," he said. "Not everyone in Asgard will speak our language as well as Odin and the rest of our visitors." A sharp tingle ran through Demon's scalp, and his brain suddenly felt as if it had stretched to twice its size. He reached up a hand to check, but his head seemed to be the normal shape it always had been.

Zeus turned to Odin.

"I'd better send my sister Demeter with you, too," he said. "She's good at crops and all that. And she's always a bit down when Persephone's with Hades. A trip to Asgard will cheer her up."

"It's settled, then," said Odin. "Now let's go and find some more of Dionysus's brew. I must persuade him to tell me how he makes it." He looked at Demon. "Go and pack, young Pandemonius. We leave at dawn."

The cloud ship was ready, rocking in the small breeze. Demon clutched a bag of the warmest things he'd been able to lay his hands on, plus the magic medicine box, his dad's pipes, and all the supplies he thought he might need. He'd even borrowed a bit of Hestia's fire, just in case.

"I hear it's cold up there," said Melanie the naiad as he was saying his goodbyes to everyone. "You might need a cloak."

"Bring me back a nice bit of meat," said the griffin, giving him a sharp peck of farewell.

"Don't worry," said Bion. "I'll take care of everyone."

As the Asgardians came down from Zeus and Hera's palace, Demon felt a tap on his shoulder. He turned around to see his dad standing there, looking uncharacteristically worried.

"You take care up there, my boy," Pan said, bending down to give him a god hug that smelled, as usual, of pungent green things, blood, and old goaty musk.

"I will, Your Dadness," he said.

But Pan hadn't finished. "Your mother had a dream about you a few nights ago. She made me swear to warn you not to go anywhere near any dark ice caves. Apparently she saw you in one—and you were in danger. I won't be able to help you in the North. It's too far for the pipes to reach if you're in trouble."

"I'll take care," Demon promised. "I've got my phoenix feather and some sandalwood with me, in case of dire emergencies. Look!" He peeled back the shoulder of his tunic to show the precious things bound against his chest with a linen bandage.

"That's good," said his dad. "Glad to see you're prepared for anything, my boy."

As Demon walked away, a little shiver trailed a cold finger down his spine. He didn't fancy the idea of a dangerous dark ice cave one little bit.

Just as he was about to go aboard the ship, Zeus beckoned him over.

"Behave yourself, and don't let me down, Stable Master," he said. "Or I may just give you to Eagle for a snack." Eagle was on his shoulder and clacked its beak menacingly, right by Demon's ear.

Demon walked onto the ship, feeling a bit lost. He stood at the stern, looking back as Olympus faded into the distance, wondering how long he'd be gone, and if Bion would manage on his own. There was no turning back now, though. He was on his own.

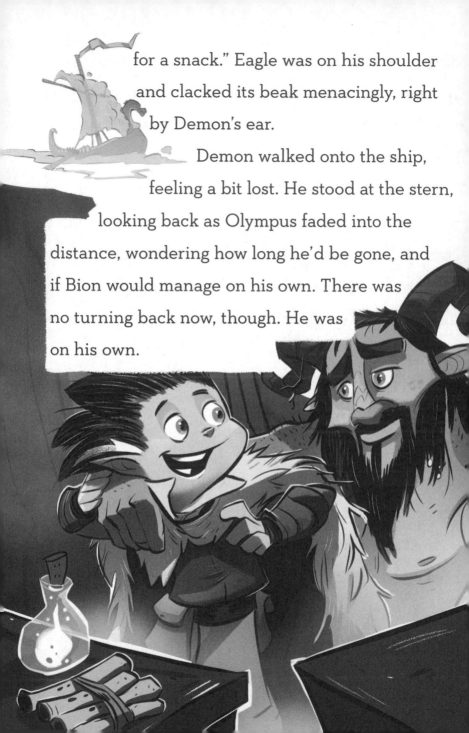

CHAPTER 5

THRUD

Demon soon left the stern and went forward to stand at the prow, which was shaped like the jaws of a ravening wolf. He'd only been there for a short while, marveling at the cloudscapes that spread out before him, when the deck started to shake, and he heard the unmistakable sound of godly footsteps behind him. Whirling around, he saw the god with the huge hammer approaching. What should he do? Should he bow? Should he fall to his knees? He didn't know how to act around these new deities at all. In the end, he compromised, going to one knee and bowing his head.

"Hey!" said the god, in a voice like the clang of swords. "None of that, young Pandemonius. Get up and face me like a man!"

Demon scrambled to his feet. "S-sorry, Your Humongous Hammeriness," he said.

"We don't go in for all that bowing and scraping in the North," the god continued, sticking out a massive iron-gloved hand toward Demon. "I'm Thor, by the way. Champion of Asgard."

Demon stuck out his own hand rather timidly. When Thor took it and shook it, though, Demon shot up high into the air and was only just caught by the cloud sails.

"By Odin's eye!" said Thor, unhooking his hammer. "I forget my own strength sometimes. Fetch, Mjolnir!"

With that he flung his hammer right at Demon. Before Demon had even had time to duck, the hammer had curled around his body like a huge hand and flown him back down to the deck at Thor's feet.

"Hmm," said Thor, looking at him. "I think I'd better get my daughter, Thrud, to sort you out when we get to Asgard. She's more your size."

The first thing that Demon noticed was that Asgard was FREEZING! It was also very gloomy. There was snow on the ground, and everything had big, fat icicles dangling from it. Although he'd already put on all the clothes he'd brought, he began to shiver almost immediately, and his toes started to go numb. The only spot of warmth he had was the phoenix feather bound to his chest, which seemed to be sending out a small pulse of heat that he was very thankful for.

All the gods and goddesses pushed past him and hurried off the cloud ship as soon as it landed, so Demon was left lost and not knowing where to go. Dragging his belongings toward the nearest building, he stumbled along, hugging himself and wishing he'd never heard of Asgard. How was he supposed to cure Goldbristle if he didn't even know where the poor beast was to be found?

Then it got worse. Snow started to fall, thick fluffy flakes of it covering his head and shoulders in seconds. Demon could see nothing. Suddenly, he heard a shout just by his left ear.

"Hey! Are you Pandemonius?"

"Y-y-yes," he tried to say, but his teeth were chattering so hard, he could hardly get the word out. A hand grabbed his arm and yanked him through a door, into a large room full of firelight. The wooden walls gave off the fragrant scent of pine, which mixed with the delicious smells coming from a large cauldron on the fire. Demon blinked the snow out of his eyes and saw a girl standing in front of him. She had hair the color of ripe corn, tied into a multitude of braids, and she wore a long cloak of blue heron feathers lined with fluffy down, over a thick woolen tunic and breeches.

"Hello," she said. "I'm Thrud Thorsdaughter. My dad sent me to take care of you." She looked Demon up and down, her eyes widening. "Are those really all the clothes you wear on Olympus?" she asked.

Demon nodded. "I-it's a lot w-warmer there," he said, through his chattering teeth. "And p-please c-call me D-Demon."

Thrud rummaged in a chest and pulled out a blanket. "Wrap this around you and help yourself to soup, Demon," she said, pointing to the cauldron. Then, with a flash of blue feathers, she was gone.

By the time Demon had eaten three bowls of soup and unfrozen his toes a bit, she was back.

"Here," she said, thrusting a bundle of clothes at him, along with a warmer pair of wool-lined boots. "Put these on. Then I'll show you around and take you to Goldbristle."

———————

It was blissful to be warm again, Demon thought, wiggling his fingers in his sheepskin mittens. He had the magic medicine box under one arm, and his sack of supplies over his shoulder. Thrud was striding ahead of him, pointing things out.

"That's Valhalla," she said as they passed a huge hall full of lights and loud laughter, with a golden tree growing outside it. "Where the heroes and the Valkyrie shield-maidens have a permanent party. I'm not allowed in there, really."

She turned toward Demon. "They can get a bit rowdy and rude," she said, grinning, and then she sighed. "All I want is to be a shield-maiden, but first I have to do a brave deed to prove myself worthy."

But Demon wasn't listening properly. He had spotted an enormous stag and a nanny goat, standing on top of the hall, nibbling on the branches of the golden tree. From the stag's golden antlers poured a glistening stream of crystal water.

"Hello," he called up. "I'm Demon from Olympus."

The stag turned its immense head. "I am Oakthorn," he said. "Nice to meet you, Demon-from-Olympus." Then he went back to nibbling.

The goat, however, leaped down. "I've heard about you," she said, butting Demon gently in the leg. "You're the one who cured my old friend Amaltheia, aren't you?" Demon nodded. "Well, mind you do the same for poor Goldbristle. I'm tired of living in the dark."

"I'll do my best," Demon said as he and Thrud walked on.

Thrud was looking at him in amazement. "Do you really know the language of all animals?" she asked.

"Yes," Demon said. "It's because of my dad, I think." And he explained about Pan being the god of the forest and the wild beasts. Just then, they passed the biggest tree Demon had ever seen in his life.

"Whoa!" he said, stopping to gaze up and up and up. "That's some tree!"

"That's Yggdrasil, the Great Ash," said Thrud, stroking the smooth gray-green bark. "It holds the worlds together." Then her eyes narrowed as a flash of flaming red darted among its branches, leaping from twig to twig.

"And that," she said with a frown, "is Ratatosk. We can all understand *him*!"

Ratatosk, Demon saw, was a huge red squirrel.

"Ooh! Ooh! A new visitor," he chattered. "I must spread the word!" And with that, he disappeared up the trunk and out of sight.

"Don't ever listen to Ratatosk's tall stories," Thrud instructed Demon. "He's a terrible tattletale and a liar, and he spreads gossip all around Asgard. Why, he even told on me once for borrowing Dad's hammer, and I was only *thinking* about it."

Demon looked at her. "Maybe he just exaggerates a bit," he said.

Thrud looked at him, a dark glint in her eyes. "Just you wait till he tells some awful fib about you, and you get threatened with scrubbing the ice off Odin's throne for it," she said.

Demon laughed. "Poseidon threatened to make me scrub salt off seaweed for a hundred years, once," he said.

"That's not as bad as the time Loki tricked me

into polishing every icicle in Asgard," she said. "He's my uncle, but you'd better watch out for him, too. Dad says he's a dangerous maniac!"

Her eyes went big and round.

"He caused a terrible fight among all the gods not long ago, and Odin All-Father had to lock him up in prison. Dad says he's threatened to take his revenge on all of Asgard."

By the time they got to Goldbristle's stable, they had traded many stories about awful things the gods had threatened them with, and were on the road to being firm friends.

As soon as Demon saw the boar, his heart sank. The beast was nearly as big as a wagon, and it was lying on its side, with tears flowing out from under its long, pale piggy eyelashes and over its long, brutal-looking tusks. It gave off a sickly greenish-golden glow, and it was groaning piteously. Frey was

sitting in the straw, stroking its hairy ears.

"He's even worse than when we left," said Frey. "The whole of Asgard is counting on you to cure him, Pandemonius."

It was a big responsibility. Demon examined Goldbristle all over, but there was nothing obvious wrong. He tapped the magic medicine box.

"Wake up, box," he said. "We have a patient." The box glowed blue all over and gave a sort of quiver.

"State nature of ailment," it said in its tinny voice.

"Goldbristle's light has gone out," Demon said. "Maybe it's a bit like the problem we had with the Cretan Bull." The Cretan Bull had lost its fire when horrible Heracles dragged it through the sea.

The box snapped open, and out whipped a series of thin bright blue tentacles with suckers all down them, which attached themselves all over Goldbristle's body, including one that probed inside his mouth.

"What are THOSE?" Demon asked. The box had never produced anything like that before.

"Upgrade 2.1, copyright Hephaestus Productions," said the box. "Now initiating test mode."

On its lid, a tiny rainbow began to whirl around and around, filling the stable with color. Demon, Frey, and Thrud waited in a breathless silence that went on, and on, and on . . .

"Hurry up, box," Demon said eventually. "We haven't got all day." With a loud *pop*, the suckers detached themselves and shot back inside.

"Running diagnostics," it said.

"What's it saying?" Thrud asked. With a start, Demon realized she couldn't understand it. He'd been speaking Asgardian without even noticing, but the box didn't have the same gift.

"Nothing important yet," he said. But as he spoke, the box spat out some blue sparks.

"Patient suffering from Porcine Skotadilitiriotitis," it said.

Demon glared at it. "Explain properly," he said.

"Also known as Piggy Darkness Poison," it said rather snarkily. "No cure ingredients in medicine cache at this time."

"What do you mean, no cure ingredients in medicine cache?" Demon asked. His stomach felt as if a big lump of snow had just landed in it. "There must be something we can do."

A blue tentacle shot out and rummaged in Demon's pack, coming out with the tiny lidded silver cauldron in which he was keeping Hestia's fire. Before Demon could do more than open his mouth, the magic medicine box had swallowed it, and then spat out a small golden bottle that glowed a bright hot orange.

"Temporary alleviation of symptoms only," said the box. "Correct cure ingredients may be available locally."

"What correct cure ingredients?" Demon asked. "And where do I find them?"

But the box had shut itself down and refused to respond.

CHAPTER 6

THE WHITE FOX

Very carefully, because his tusks were sharp,
Demon tipped half the potion down Goldbristle's
throat, thinking furiously. The box hadn't said there
wasn't a cure—just that the right ingredients might
be available locally. That meant that there must be
something here in Asgard—he just had to find it.

As the last drop of fiery liquid dribbled in,
Goldbristle started to glow a little brighter, then
brighter still, till the stall was bathed in a warm
golden light.

Thrud clapped. "Look, Uncle Frey! He's done it!" she crowed.

"Well done, Pandemonius," said the god as Goldbristle lumbered to its feet and grunted.

Demon turned to look up at the great boar. "How are you feeling?" he asked.

"Not so good," said Goldbristle. "My light still feels as if it's all dissolving into nothing."

"Did you eat or drink something bad?"

The bristly head shook from side to side. "No, but my dreams are full of darkness eating the world," it said.

Demon met the round black eyes, shiny as beetle wings and framed in long, thick lashes.

"I'll find a cure for you if it's the last thing I do," he promised.

He turned to Frey. "I don't think you'd better take Goldbristle out just yet, Your Golden Magnificence," he said.

Frey frowned, and it was like the sun going behind a cloud. "Why not? You've cured him, haven't you? He will keep on getting brighter, won't he?"

Demon shook his head. "It's only temporary," he said. "I don't know how long it will last. He might go out again at any minute."

Frey frowned again. "Then I must take advantage of his light while I can," he said. "Help me harness him up."

Reluctantly, Demon did as he was told.

"I'm sorry," he whispered to Goldbristle as the enormous beast lumbered out of the stable, with Frey in the golden chariot behind it. But the shining boar was already rising into the sky and didn't hear him.

Immediately, the whole of Asgard began to sparkle like one big diamond. Demon had to half close his eyes till they adjusted.

"Isn't it beautiful?" said Thrud, clapping her hands and leaping about. She picked up a big handful of soft snow, shaped it into a ball, and threw it at him.

"*Oof!*" said Demon as it hit him right in the face.

"Score one for Team Thrud," she shrieked, lobbing another one at him. Demon ducked, scooped up his own snowball, and threw it.

"Right in the hood," said Thrud, laughing and shaking snow off herself. "Score one for Team Demon!" But just as Demon was starting to get into the swing of things, it all went horribly wrong. Suddenly, the bright diamond light began to dim, and as he looked up, he saw Goldbristle lurch and fall from the sky.

"Oh no!" Demon said, and began to run.

With a crash, the boar bounced off the corner of a roof, leaving it in splintered ruins, and dropped into a snowdrift. Frey leaped clear of the golden chariot as it shattered on the icy ground. It was as if night had fallen all in a minute.

Demon didn't want to say *I told you so* to a god, but he felt like it, as he rubbed bruise-flower ointment into all Goldbristle's sore bits and bandaged the leg he'd sprained in the fall. Frey was fussing around, getting in Demon's way as he worked, and he just wished Frey would go away.

"It's all my fault," the handsome god said.

Demon closed his lips around a *yes it is*, keeping it in with difficulty.

Frey put a hand on his shoulder. "You can fix him, can't you?" he asked, as Demon fed Goldbristle the other half of his medicine. This time the boar's glow was much fainter, and he was groaning piteously again.

"I hope so," he said. "But you can't take Goldbristle out again, you know. He was lucky he didn't get hurt much worse than he did."

"I know," said Frey, looking guilty.

He wasn't the least bit like most of the gods Demon knew—he wasn't scary at all.

"I think I'm missing something," Demon said. "Have you ever heard of something like a darkness poison? Because that's what my box thinks is wrong with him, and I can't find anything else that fits."

Frey sighed. "No," he said. "I haven't. But I'll ask the other Asgardians if they have. I'll go right now."

A little while later, there was a patter of feet on

the roof of the stable, then two heavy thumps and the screech of claws slipping on ice. When Demon heard the thud of a falling body hitting the ground and a loud shriek, he rushed outside.

Ratatosk the squirrel was sitting on his haunches, nursing one of his front paws. He was chattering angrily at two giant silver-black wolves, whose eyes shone like fire. They were on their bellies, stalking toward him with their tongues hanging out.

"Squirrel snacks," growled one.

"Spy supper," howled the other.

"Hey!" said Demon, stepping between them. "Leave him alone. Can't you see he's hurt?"

The wolves slunk away, snarling, before Demon even had a chance to find out who they were.

"What have you done to yourself?" he asked the squirrel. "Let me see."

Ratatosk held out his paw, which was dripping

with blood. "Horrid creatures," he said. "Chasing poor Ratatosk like that."

"Who were those wolves, anyway?" Demon asked.

"The All-Father's nasty pets, Ravenous and Greedy. They eat all his food and don't leave even a crumb for little Ratatosk." The squirrel whimpered. "Poor Ratatosk, nobody likes him."

"Well, I do," said Demon, fetching a bandage and some ointment from his bag. "You seem like someone who knows everything. Maybe you can help me." As he cleaned and dressed the paw, he explained about needing to find the right ingredients to cure Goldbristle.

"But I have no idea where to start," he finished.

"Ratatosk will help," said the squirrel. "Ratatosk will run very fast up and down the Great Ash and ask all his friends, even the scary worm. Ratatosk can find out *anything*," he boasted.

"Don't run too fast," said Demon. "You take care of that paw, now." But the squirrel had already gone.

———◆———

Demon spent the next two days looking after Goldbristle and racking his brains for a cure. Thrud kept him company sometimes, but she wasn't a big help since she knew nothing about medicine. The magic medicine box couldn't seem to give him any more useful information, and his life wasn't made any easier by Ravenous and Greedy, who had taken to following him around with their tongues hanging out, threatening to bite big chunks out of him unless he made some progress—fast. And the All-Father's two ravens, Thought and Memory, were always hovering overhead, watching him. Altogether, it made him very nervous. What if he couldn't find a cure? Would Odin freeze him into an icicle statue and use him for spear practice? Or would he just let the wolves and ravens tear him apart and eat him?

Demon wasn't getting much sleep, either. That first night, Thrud had turned up at the stable again and shown him to his room, which was a tiny cubbyhole above Valhalla, lined with cozy sheepskins. Unfortunately, it was very noisy indeed, what with the warriors and the Valkyrie shield-maidens below him drinking mead and singing rude songs that made him blush. They also seemed to have a game where they threw axes into the ceiling. One had crashed through the floorboard by his foot, making him huddle in a corner till it was time to get up. In the end, he'd used some wax from his medicine bag to block his ears, and hoped that the axes would keep on missing him.

The only good news was that Demeter was somehow helping to make things grow again. She'd set up a huge greenhouse made of some kind of ice panels that didn't melt, and had lit it with special lamps she'd borrowed from Helios. It shone like a lone beacon amid the darkness of Asgard.

By the third night, Demon was nearly in despair. He'd made no progress, and Frey wasn't being any help at all. Apparently none of the gods and goddesses had ever heard of a darkness poison. Even Ratatosk hadn't been able to find out anything. And then, with a great clangor of bells and horns, the alarm sounded.

"Frost Giant attack! Frost Giant attack!" shouted a great voice, and with a clatter of armor and swords and running feet, Asgard emptied. As Demon watched, a posse of Valkyrie shield-maidens flew past him, along with a band of warrior heroes, then Thor with his hammer at his belt, and a one-handed god Demon didn't recognize. Soon all was silent.

"What am I going to do?" he groaned into his

hands as he sat alone on his pile of sheepskins. Even Thrud, it seemed, had deserted him.

With a pitter-patter of delicate black-tipped paws, a white fox trotted into the room. It had eyes as red as rubies, and fur as soft as a cloud.

"I can help," it said, sitting down in front of him and curling its tail around its feet.

"Who are you?" Demon asked. "Did Ratatosk send you?"

The fox cocked its head to one side, bright eyes watching him as its tongue lolled out in a foxy laugh. "You may call me Trixietoes," it said. "And let's just say a little birdie told me you needed some information."

Demon leaned forward eagerly. "I definitely do need information.

Can you tell me how to cure Goldbristle?"

"I can't," said Trixietoes, "but I can take you to someone who can. Have you heard of Fafnir?"

Demon shook his head.

"Shame on you," said the fox lightly. "Not heard of the great ice dragon, Fafnir? The terror of the world? The collector of stories? Fafnir of the fearless soul, who guards his hoard of gold and gems with a fire so cold it burns?"

"No," said Demon a little sourly. "I'm not from here."

"Never mind. Fafnir knows everything. He will be able to find a cure for your little piggy friend. But the way is dark and dangerous. I can lead you there for a price."

"What price?" Demon asked. This fox was not giving him a good feeling, and he wasn't sure he trusted it.

"Now, where would be the fun in telling you

that?" said Trixietoes. "Are you coming or not?"

"Coming," said Demon, scrambling into his clothes and boots. He'd been in dark and dangerous places before. And after all, how bad could a fox's price be? It would probably be like the griffin and just want some extra meat. If it got him the ingredients he needed to cure Goldbristle, it would be worth it.

CHAPTER 7

SVARTALFHEIM

As Trixietoes led him through the back ways of Asgard, through narrow alleyways and then into a dark tunnel that led steeply downward, Demon suddenly remembered his dad's warning. *Don't go anywhere near any dark ice caves.* All at once, his stomach was full of icy prickles that flowed up over his shoulders and down his spine.

"Hey!" he called. "Trixietoes! Where, exactly, are you taking me?" But the fox had disappeared, and as Demon spoke, rough hands seized him.

"Help!" Demon tried to call, fighting with everything he had against the dark-cloaked figures that surrounded him. But despite his best efforts, a large sack was jammed over his head and body, and a sweet-smelling cloth was forced inside the sack. Demon felt his head begin to spin, and his cries slurred into mumbles. He was picked up and slung over a bony shoulder, and then he knew nothing more.

***

Demon woke to find himself in pitch darkness, tied up hand and foot. His head felt as if it had been stuffed with scratchy burnt grass, and his mouth tasted like hundred-year-old hundred-armed monster dribble. There was a strange buzzing noise, right by his ear, as if a fly was hovering there. He tried to move, but as soon as he did, whatever was holding him burned his wrists and ankles with a hiss of freezing air.

"Oh, I wouldn't do that if I were you," said an amused voice close beside him. "I'd hate for you to lose an extremity."

Demon cracked open an eye and peered into the darkness, but he couldn't see anyone or anything.

"W-who are you?" he whispered, trying not to let his voice shake with terror.

"Well, I suppose I *should* introduce myself properly," said the voice, which had now moved in front of him. Gradually a sickly green light began to glow out of the walls, revealing a tall, thin figure with a pointy beard and a silver helmet with curly ram's horns attached to it. Demon recognized him at once. It was the god he'd noticed right at the back of the line of gods and goddesses when the cloud ship arrived on Olympus. The one who'd been so hard to see properly.

"But you're a god . . . ," he gasped.

"Yes," the god agreed. "I am, indeed. The god Loki, to be precise, Master Pandemonius. But if you like, you could call me Trixietoes." In a dazzling flash of light, the white fox reappeared where the god had been, and then disappeared again to leave Loki standing there, a wild, wicked look of triumph on his face.

Tricksy, indeed, Demon thought, though he didn't say it aloud, and with a sickening lurch of his heart, he remembered what Thrud had said about her uncle Loki. *He's a dangerous maniac... He's threatened to take his revenge on all of Asgard.*

"Why have you brought me here?" Demon asked.

"Oh, that," said Loki carelessly. "Well, I couldn't have you mending old Goldbristle, now, could I? After I'd gone to so much trouble to poison him, I mean."

Demon was so furious that he lunged for the god, then hissed with pain as his shackles burned him again.

"How could you?" he yelled. The anger seemed to have chased all the fear out of him. "What has poor Goldbristle ever done to you?"

"Well, nothing, really," said Loki. "But I was annoyed with Odin and the others, so I decided to take their light away." His lips curled away from his teeth in an ugly snarl. "Nobody puts me in prison and gets away with it."

Demon thought furiously. If he could flatter Loki into telling him what poison he'd used, maybe somehow he could escape and find a cure. He forced an admiring look onto his face.

"So you didn't just trick me," he said, opening his eyes very wide. "You tricked all the gods, as well. Nobody has a clue how you did it, so you must be very clever. I've never had a failure with curing a beast before—but you definitely beat me. However did you do it?"

Loki laughed evilly. "They don't call me the Father of Lies for nothing," he said. "But it wasn't easy. I had to steal a drop of darkness, right from the heart of the earth. Once a creature of light has eaten that, nothing will cure it but a drop of old Fafnir's blood, dripped onto an ice diamond, then ground up and mixed with some Fenrir wolf spit. Have fun finding *those*! Oh, wait . . ." He paused for effect, a sneer on his face. "You can't. Because you're going to be locked up down here FOREVER! Have fun with the dark elves, little healer!"

And with another evil laugh, he shimmered into a bright green fly and buzzed off through the bars of the silver gate that now appeared in the wall.

Immediately, two terrifying figures appeared outside. As they unlocked the gate and entered his dungeon, Demon cowered back, knowing that these must be the dark elves that had captured him. They wore black hoods that covered their faces, so all he could see were two pairs of white eyes with red pupils, and the bony green hands that now reached out for him, their pointed nails filthy and clotted with what looked like dark red blood.

"Leave me alone!" he cried, flinching as his shackles burned him for a third time.

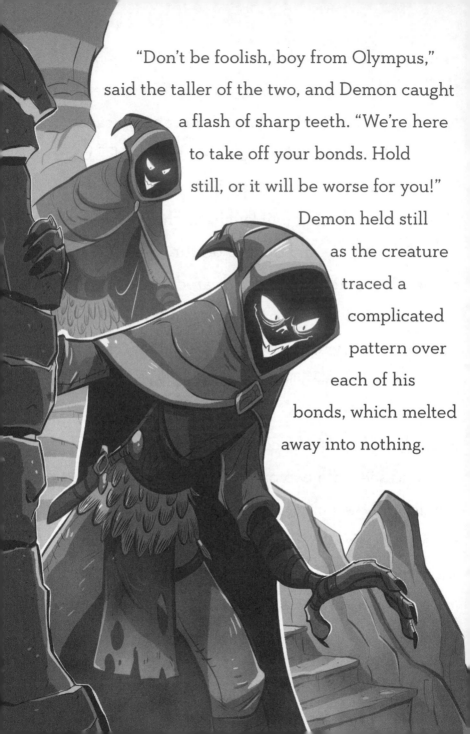

"Don't be foolish, boy from Olympus," said the taller of the two, and Demon caught a flash of sharp teeth. "We're here to take off your bonds. Hold still, or it will be worse for you!" Demon held still as the creature traced a complicated pattern over each of his bonds, which melted away into nothing.

"Here," said the other, shoving a stone plate at him that held a glowing mound of something black and slimy, together with a mug of oily water. "The best Svartalfheim cuisine! Enjoy!" It chuckled like a stream running over knives.

"I-is that where I am, then?" Demon asked, trying to keep his voice steady.

"Why, yes, young master. It is. And we are your personal jailers, Grod and Cinder." The creature bowed with a mocking flourish.

"Pleased to meet you," said Demon stoutly. Maybe he could persuade them to let him go if he was polite enough.

"Ooh!" said the one he thought was Cinder. "Listen to its lovely manners!"

The other dark elf put its face near Demon. "Lovely manners don't open locks," Grod hissed. "So don't think you'll get around us that way."

Faster than a midnight whirlwind, they spun away from him and out through the gate, locking it behind them.

"Bye for now," they jeered. "Don't go anywhere!" And then they were gone.

Demon walked around his dungeon, trying not to panic. There was a kind of rough pallet of rags in one corner, but there were no windows, and when he touched the silver bars, they threw him backward to the other side of the cell in a welter of scarlet sparks. He hit the glowing green wall with a thump and slid down it, landing on his bottom on the rough stone floor, trying to control his breathing, but it was no good.

"Help!" he screamed angrily. "Odin! Thor! Thrud! Someone, help me!" But all he heard as he lay there, choking back tears of rage, were echoes of his own voice, and then silence.

Eventually he sat up, wiping his nose with his hand. Somewhere in the scuffle back in Asgard, he had lost his sheepskin mittens, and now his hands were freezing. He tucked them under his armpits to try to warm them.

Come on, Demon, he thought. *There has to be some way to get out of this.* He looked in the pouch at his waist. His dad's pipes were no good—he knew that. Olympus was too far away for them to reach. And there was nothing else in the pouch but a few pinches of dried herbs, an acorn, a scrap of parchment he'd made some notes on, and a stub of charcoal.

Then all at once he became aware of a pulse of warmth in the middle of his chest.

"Of course! The phoenix feather!" he gasped, suddenly remembering that he had it with him. But then he looked around his cold, dank dungeon, and his momentary joy ran out of his toes like water.

The phoenix had told him to throw the feather into a sandalwood fire if he was ever in great danger—and then help would come. Well, if ever he'd needed help, it was now. But how was he going to light a fire in this dark, damp place? There were no torches, not even any light except for the green glow in the walls, and what remained of Hestia's fire was back in Asgard, eaten up by the magical medicine box. He didn't even have a flint with him to strike a spark.

"How could I have been so stupid?" he groaned. "I'm a total idiot." What hope did he have now of escaping this terrible place?

CHAPTER 8

THE BLOOD OF FAFNIR

Demon looked around his dungeon one more time, just in case, but again he saw nothing that might help. He stumbled over to the rag pallet in despair and sat down. Right away, there was a cracking sound, and he leaped up again with a yelp. He'd sat on something sharp. Rubbing the bruise on his bottom, he lifted up the rags, which smelled horrible, like something had died on them. Underneath was a spike of shiny black rock with the tip broken off. That must have been what snapped. Demon looked at it. Maybe, just maybe, it was the answer to his prayers.

Scrabbling frantically with his cold fingers, he picked it up and looked at it, then scraped it experimentally against the rough gray rock of the floor. It made a satisfying scritching sound.

Hands trembling with excitement, he fumbled under his clothes for the little pouch of sandalwood shavings and the feather. Then he ripped a bit of sheep's wool off the lining of his coat and made it into a tiny ball, putting some of the sandalwood on top.

Scritch-scratch-scritch went the black stone against the gray rock. Demon could feel it getting warm.

"Come on!" he said. "Make a spark!" But however hard he willed it to come, no spark appeared.

Despair settled into him like a deep gray fog,

but just as he was gloomily gathering up the fire ingredients and the feather again, he heard a tiny pattering sound and a loud sniff. Quickly, he shoved everything inside his coat. Someone—or something—was here, and he wasn't going to risk his one hope of escape being discovered.

"Who's that?" he whispered, hoping it wasn't Cinder and Grod again.

There was a squeak, and outside the bars appeared the furry red figure of the squirrel, Ratatosk. Demon felt a great wave of relief crash over him.

"Oh, thank Zeus!" he said. "I thought nobody was ever going to find me down here."

"Ratatosk was clever," said the squirrel.

"Ratatosk saw you go off with the wicked Loki fox and followed."

"Well, I'm glad you did, Ratatosk," Demon said gratefully. "You are definitely the cleverest squirrel in the whole world. Now, can you get me out of here?"

The squirrel shook his head. "Ratatosk can't open elf locks. They bite."

Demon felt his excitement drain away, but then he had an idea. "Well, if you can't open the lock, could you find me a bit of fire? Maybe a torch or something?"

The squirrel cocked his head to one side. "Maybe," he said. "Ratatosk will try." And with that, he scampered off.

Demon paced around the dungeon while he waited, stamping his feet to keep warm. It was so cold now that his breath was freezing into tiny cloud crystals in front of his face. Sooner than he'd hoped, he heard the patter of paws again. Ratatosk was back and, even better, he held in his paws a flickering torch that trailed foul-smelling black smoke.

"Ratatosk stole the fire!" he chattered. "It nearly burned his tail!"

"Can you pass it through the bars without touching them?" Demon asked. He didn't want Ratatosk to be hurt.

Eventually, with great care and a few near misses, Demon held the torch in his hands. He crouched down, looking into Ratatosk's inquisitive black eyes.

"Will you do one more thing for me?" he asked. "Will you go and tell Thrud what's happened and where I am? Maybe if I can't get out by myself, Thor could come and rescue me when he's back from fighting giants."

The squirrel's ears drooped. "Thrud doesn't like

Ratatosk," he said. "She won't believe him."

Demon thought for a minute, then leaned the torch carefully against the wall and pulled out the scrap of parchment and the charcoal from his pouch.

"Yes, she will," he said, scrubbing out his notes and drawing a series of pictures on the smeary surface. He slipped it under the bars. "Give her this."

As the squirrel scampered off again, Demon could only hope that Thrud would be able to interpret his scrawls. He hadn't dared write anything, in case she couldn't understand it.

Carefully he built his tiny fire again and set light to it. Once it was ablaze, he threw in the precious gold-and-red feather.

"Phoenix!" he cried. "Come to my aid!"

There was a great whoosh of flame that lit up the dark dungeon. The sickly green glow of the walls turned blue and began to glitter strangely, and then, with a high, sweet burst of song, the phoenix was there, and the fire disappeared, leaving behind a pleasant fragrance in the air.

"How can I help, O protector of the phoenix?" it said in its beautiful voice.

Demon explained about Loki and how Goldbristle had been poisoned.

"And now I need to get an ice diamond, and find this dragon Fafnir, and get a drop of his blood," he said, all in a rush. "Oh, and also some spit from a wolf called Fenrir. But before I do any of that, I have to get out of here."

The phoenix looked at him. "That's quite some task, young healer. Getting out of here won't be easy, and if I know Fafnir, he won't be too eager to give you his blood. But the ice diamond I can help with. There are plenty here."

"Where?" Demon asked, but the bird was

already pecking at one of the strange glitters in the walls.

Just as the phoenix dropped a sparkly white pebble at his feet, Demon became aware of harsh shouts outside, and the sound of running feet.

"Oh no!" he said, picking up the pebble, which felt like a drop of pure frost in his hand, and putting it in his pouch. "The dark elves are coming!"

"Then hold on to my tail, Pandemonius, and don't let go, whatever you do!"

Demon grabbed the phoenix's long, fiery tail and hoped that he wouldn't get burnt. Though the flames licked and curled around his hands and arms, it just felt pleasantly warm.

"How do we—" he started, but the bird was already flying straight upward toward the ceiling.

"Wha—"

His voice cut out as the phoenix flew *into* the stone, pulling Demon behind it. It was the oddest

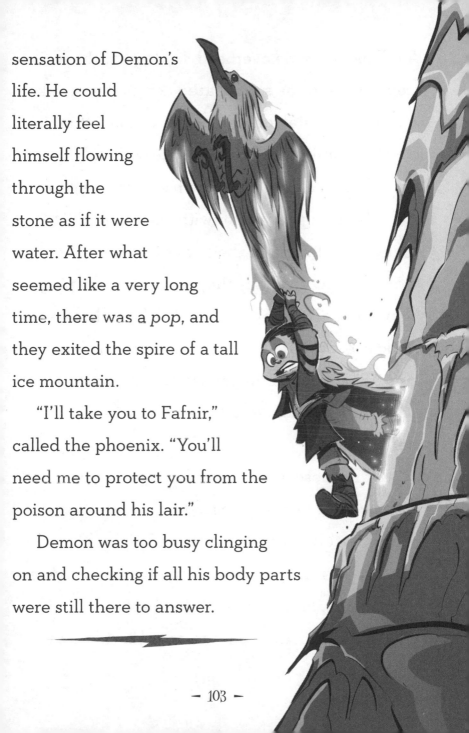

sensation of Demon's life. He could literally feel himself flowing through the stone as if it were water. After what seemed like a very long time, there was a *pop*, and they exited the spire of a tall ice mountain.

"I'll take you to Fafnir," called the phoenix. "You'll need me to protect you from the poison around his lair."

Demon was too busy clinging on and checking if all his body parts were still there to answer.

A full moon shone overhead, lighting up the white ice below, and the stars blazed across the sky like a string of crystal jewels. Demon was just thinking how beautiful it was, when the ice suddenly became gray and cracked, with smoke rising from it. Pools of stagnant water with what looked like sticky black fungus at their edges lay here and there, and occasionally they made loud slurping *blop* noises. The gray stretched as far as his eyes could see, eventually rising into a gigantic black mountain wreathed in plumes of noxious steam. Demon had a nasty feeling he knew where they were headed.

As they descended toward a jagged cave entrance, the phoenix began to glow, emitting a pale rose-colored mist that twined around Demon, who had begun to cough and splutter as the fumes hit his lungs. Immediately he felt better.

"Stay within my mist," the phoenix called as

they landed. "It will protect you. And let me do the talking."

The first thing Demon noticed was the terrible smell. The second thing he noticed was the glittering heap of gold and gems, which slid and crunched beneath his feet like autumn leaves on a frozen pond.

Unfortunately, the third thing he noticed was the pair of eyes high above him. The eyes were huge and round as millstones, and green, with a golden slit right in the middle.

"Who dares to disturb Fafnir?" came a great grumble of a voice.

"I am the phoenix of the Mountains of Burning Sand," it said. "And I bring my companion, Pandemonius of Olympus, to ask a boon!"

"A boon?" Fafnir bellowed. "You lie! You are robbers and thieves, come to steal my hoard!" A gout of pure white flame roared out of its mouth,

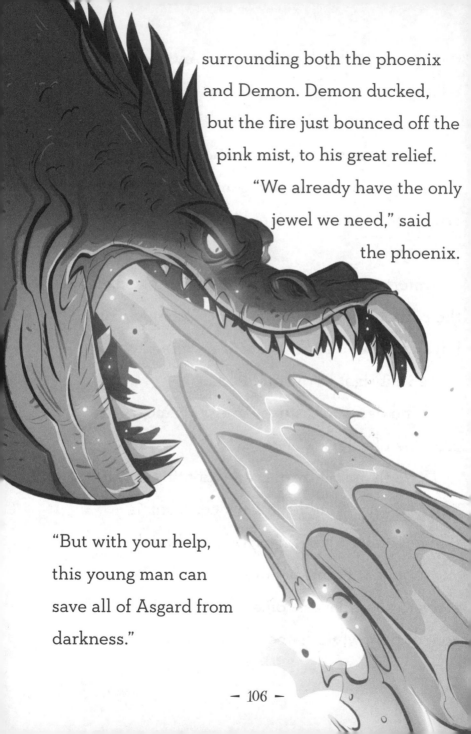

surrounding both the phoenix
and Demon. Demon ducked,
but the fire just bounced off the
pink mist, to his great relief.
"We already have the only
jewel we need," said
the phoenix.

"But with your help,
this young man can
save all of Asgard from
darkness."

"How so?" asked Fafnir, sounding intrigued, and Demon remembered that Trixietoes had called the dragon a collector of stories.

"My companion will explain."

So Demon cleared his throat and told the story of Goldbristle and Loki once more. As soon as he got to the part about Loki, Fafnir roared again, so that the very rocks around them shook.

"That thief, that renegade, that black-hearted weasel-tosser of a god! So he's responsible for the darkness, is he? How dare he?"

More white flames shot out, toward the ceiling this time, which sprouted smoking icicles as big as stalactites. The dragon lowered its pale spiked head, stretching out its neck toward Demon,

who tried not to breathe, or to look at the shreds of rotten meat caught in the beast's arm-length teeth.

"Very well," said the dragon. "What do you need from me, youngling?"

"Just one drop of your blood on this ice diamond, O wise and mighty Fafnir," said Demon, pulling it from his pouch and holding it out.

Delicately for such a huge creature, Fafnir lifted one gigantic foreleg, extended one long curved talon, and pierced his other leg. A stream of steaming blood ran out, hissing as it hit the gold beneath. Demon willed his hand not to tremble as the talon hovered over his fingers, one drop of scarlet gore hanging from its tip. It fell, hitting the ice diamond square in the middle, sinking in immediately, and turning the jewel as red as fire. Quickly, Demon stowed it in his pouch again.

"Thank you, great one," he said, bowing low. "Now all I have to get is some spit from Fenrir, and

Goldbristle can be cured."

Fafnir let out a bellow of dragonish laughter.

"Drool from the mad wolf?" he roared. "I wish you luck with that, my young friend. Be careful you do not suffer the same fate as poor Tyr One-Hand. Now, go. I feel a hunger coming upon me. I wouldn't want to mistake you for dinner."

Demon didn't wait to be told twice. He grabbed the phoenix's tail again, and soon they were soaring through the air toward Asgard.

"I will have to leave you now," the phoenix called, swooping down to land outside Goldbristle's stable. "I must return to my mountains and sing the fire devils their nightly lullaby."

"Thank you for saving me," Demon said. But his only answer was a second phoenix feather swirling down to land at his feet. He picked it up and stowed it carefully against his chest, where it made a small comforting warmth against his heart.

CHAPTER 9

THE MAD WOLF

Almost as soon as he had landed, Thrud came skidding around the corner.

"Where have you *been*?" she yelled. "Ratatosk just told me some parcel of lies about you being kept prisoner down in Svartalfheim. And what does *this* mean?" She waved the bit of parchment at him.

"Ratatosk wasn't telling a parcel of lies," Demon said, suddenly angry. "You should give him some credit. And that," he said, grabbing the piece of parchment, "was me trying to ask your dad to come and rescue me. But don't worry. I got out, anyway, no thanks to you."

He turned to go into Goldbristle's stable, seething.

The boar was lying on its side, its light almost gone, and Demon's anger evaporated as quickly as it had come. He ran over to the enormous creature and reached up to stroke its bristly head.

"Don't worry, old chap," he said. "I've nearly got a cure. I just have to get some Fenrir spit, and you'll be right as rain in no time."

He heard a tiny cough behind him and turned to see Thrud standing there, looking a bit sheepish.

"I'm sorry I yelled at you," she said. "But I was just so worried when you disappeared. I've been all alone since everyone went off to fight the giants. And I'm sorry I didn't believe Ratatosk. Were you really captured by Loki and the dark elves? How on earth did you get out?"

Demon told Thrud the whole story. By the end, her mouth had turned into a big round O, and if her eyes had gotten any bigger, they would have popped out of her head.

"You went to see *Fafnir*?" she gasped. "How are you even still alive?"

"Well, it was all because of the phoenix, really," Demon said modestly. He looked at her and sighed. "But now I have to find Fenrir. Do you know where he is?"

Thrud nodded slowly. "I do," she said. "Ever since the beast bit off Uncle Tyr's hand, he's been chained up on an island in the middle of our lake. Dad says that the wolf is quite mad—and I'm forbidden to go anywhere near him. But I know how to get there."

Even though there was nobody around, she lowered her voice. "You know how I was telling you about having to do a brave deed to prove myself worthy of being a shield-maiden? Well, I'm thinking that if I row you out to Fenrir's island, that would count as one, wouldn't it?"

"I should think so," said Demon. "Though I wonder if he really is mad. Perhaps it's just that he's been left tied up and alone."

Thrud gave him a long look. "Trust me," she said. "He's mad. Odin loves wolves, and he only tied Fenrir up because Fenrir's meant to kill him. Now, come along, hurry up." She cocked an ear, listening. "Everyone will be coming back from fighting the giants soon. We need to steal a boat right now. With any luck they'll all be either feasting or asleep by the time we get back."

Thrud, it turned out, was almost as good at sneaking around Asgard as the white fox had been. The difference was, though, that this time Demon knew he wasn't going to be kidnapped.

Soon they were creeping onto a long pier, jutting out into a lake so big that Demon couldn't even guess where the far shore was in the darkness. A series of long, low boats with high prows were tied up alongside.

"Come on," said Thrud, climbing into a boat made of some kind of pale wood and shaped like a swan. "Let's take this one. It belongs to Idunn. She'll never notice. That goddess of yours—Demeter—has got her working in that big greenhouse, trying to make her apple trees come into fruit."

Demon rather hoped Demeter wouldn't notice them, either. He didn't want her reporting back any trouble to Zeus—though she hadn't exactly taken any notice of anything he'd done so far. But since getting the spit from Fenrir was a key part of getting Goldbristle better, he thought he'd probably be forgiven.

"Get comfortable and keep quiet," Thrud

ordered him. "We don't want the lake serpents to hear us." She pushed off and started to row, with long, steady strokes that hardly broke the surface of the still water. Demon lay there, looking up at the stars and wondering why they were so different from the ones that shone above Olympus. Then he let out a small gasp. On the far horizon, waves of color were dancing—billowing curtains of pale green and pink and blue moving across the sky. Thrud saw him looking.

"The Nimble Dancers," she whispered very quietly. "Some say they've been up there since before the All-Father himself." Then, all at once, she let out a muffled scream and shook her oars, making the boat rock dangerously. Demon saw a ripple in the water, and a dozen slimy heads broke the surface on each side. They twined around the oar blades, biting and snapping with their sharp needle teeth.

"Lake serpents," Thrud said, her voice slightly desperate. "They never give up till they've eaten their prey. I'll try to fight them off." She pulled out a small dagger from her belt and bent toward the beasts on the left-hand side.

But Demon had already pulled out his dad's pipes. He put them to his lips and started to play. Immediately, all the serpents went limp and slid off the oars, slipping back into the water and disappearing below.

"Phew!" he said. "I wasn't sure these were going to work up here."

After what seemed like hours had passed, the island loomed up before them. Thrud beached the boat on a small point of frozen sand.

"This way," she said, unsheathing her dagger again. "And whatever you do, don't get anywhere near his jaws."

"No stabbing," said Demon sternly. He wasn't allowing any beast to be hurt on his watch. "I'll use my pipes again if I have to, but I have to get near enough to collect some of his drool, or there's no point in us being here."

Thrud rolled her eyes. "I said I would do a brave deed, not a stupid one. I promise I won't stab him unless I have to, though," she said, and Demon had to be content with that.

The path wound up and up through the rocky cliffs, and Demon was out of breath by the time they reached the top. When he got there, he saw a gigantic round boulder set into the earth, with what looked like a ghostly greenish-gold silk ribbon wound around and around it, and anchored to a tall stone post that had been driven right through the middle of it. Attached to the other end of the ribbon was the biggest wolf he'd ever seen, fast asleep and curled around the boulder as if it were a tiny pebble.

"How on earth does that little ribbon hold such a big creature?" he whispered with no more than a breath of sound in Thrud's ear.

"It's stronger than it looks," she whispered back. "Fenrir broke three huge chains before they tried this one. Dad says the dwarfs made it out of six things: the sound of a cat's paws, a giantess's beard, the roots of a mountain, the sinews of a bear, the breath of a fish, and bird spit."

Demon wasn't sure most of those things even existed, but as he himself had had to capture a maiden's sigh and the high and low notes from a lyre to cure Hades's pet three-headed dog, Cerberus, he wasn't going to argue. He didn't like the fact that Fenrir was tied up at all, though, and when they got closer, he started to get really angry. He seized Thrud by the arm.

"What did they do *that* for?" he whispered, pointing. The poor beast's jaws were pinned open with a long golden sword, so that his tongue rolled out onto the ground. Demon could see that there would be no trouble collecting drool—streams of it were running out of Fenrir's mouth and dribbling onto the ground with a sound like a trickling drain.

"To stop him from biting, I suppose," Thrud replied. "But it doesn't look very nice, does it?"

"It does *not*. And I'm going to get it out."

Before Thrud could do more than hiss a frantic *no* at him, Demon strode forward, ready to help the poor creature or die trying. But as he did so, his foot landed on a pile of dry heather and sank into it with a sharp *crack*.

Fenrir was awake immediately, leaping up with a long, wavering *arroooo*, and lunging at them, his eyes fiery red. His jaws flung drool and foam around in bloody red strings. Although Demon could understand every beast alive, he couldn't make head or tail of what Fenrir was saying. It just sounded like insane gibberish, apart from two words: "Kill Odin."

Then he started to choke as the green-gold ribbon seemed to tighten around his throat, and the words and gibberish were cut off into a kind of strangled gargle.

"Quick!" shouted Thrud. "Play your pipes."

Demon already had them in his hand, and jamming them against his lips, he played his dad's special emergency twiddle.

Nothing happened at first, and then, very, very slowly, the great wolf collapsed. His eyes closed, and he lay utterly still.

"Oh, poor thing," Demon said, his voice all choked up. "Poor, poor Fenrir." Slowly, he walked over to the huge sleeping body and tried to pry the gaping jaws farther open so that he could get the sword free. But he couldn't do it by himself.

"Help me," he begged Thrud, and with her assistance, he eased out the sword and threw it as far away as he could. It hit the frozen ground with a mournful clang that echoed the one in Demon's heart. The moment he'd laid his hands on the beast, he'd felt the wrongness in him, like veins of poisonous red and black hate invisible to the eye. For the first time in his life, he knew there was nothing he could do to cure this creature. Fenrir was truly, completely lost to madness.

With tears rolling down his cheeks, Demon

pulled up clumps of dry, dead grass and tucked them around the great wolf's body, making a kind of cozy nest for him. Thrud was crying, too, sitting on the boulder beside the sleeping beast and stroking his ragged black ears.

Finally, Demon was done. He pulled out the corked jar he'd brought from his pouch and scooped up some of the red-tinged drool.

"Sleep is the only thing I can give him," he said as they walked back down the cliff path. "I don't know how long the spell will last. It might be forever, if I don't play the notes to wake him up."

"Then may he sleep till Ragnarok and the end of the world," she said, sniffing. "And may his dreams be full of light."

What followed was a sad and silent journey back to Asgard, but when they got there, it was ablaze with candles and the sound of celebration.

CHAPTER 10

THE STOLEN HAMMER

Even though he now had the last ingredient he needed to make Goldbristle's medicine, Demon felt miserable leaving Fenrir. Maybe if he'd been able to call Morpheus, the spirit of dreams, he might have been able to help, as he had with the man-eating mares, but Demon somehow doubted it. Fenrir was no ordinary beast. He was the brother of Jormungand, the scary worm who coiled around the roots of the world tree, and of Hel, goddess of the dead, Thrud had told him.

"So he's not just an immortal—he's a half god," she finished as they were walking back to Goldbristle's stable, avoiding staggering knots of warriors on their way to feast in Valhalla. Demon gave a deep sigh.

"Well, at least I get to cure Goldbristle now," he said. As soon as they were inside, he got out his mortar and pestle, dropped in the ice diamond, and started to pound on it.

"Better . . . turn . . . it . . . into . . . dust . . . before . . . I . . . add . . . the . . . Fenrir . . . spit," he panted as he brought down the pestle over and over again. Nothing happened. The ice diamond didn't even have the tiniest crack in it.

"Here, let me have a go," said Thrud. But she couldn't turn it into dust, either.

"I know," said Demon. "We'll get my magic medicine box to do it."

He tapped it sharply on the lid. "Wake up, box!

I've found the ingredients we need," he said.

With a blue flicker and a buzzing noise, the box came to life. "Insert item," it said in its tinny voice, and a round, mouthlike hole opened in its lid. Demon plucked the ice diamond out of the mortar and poked it into the hole. After a few clonks and a loud, screechy whir, the ice diamond came flying back out again, nearly hitting him in the eye.

"Pulverization program damage alert," it said. "Initiating repairs in lockdown mode." Immediately the rainbow wheel began to spin on all four sides, and the hole snapped shut.

Demon felt like screaming. "Now what are we going to do?" he said. "If we can't crush the diamond, we can't make the medicine."

Goldbristle groaned. "I'm going to die, then," he grunted piteously.

"No, you aren't," Demon said, his voice fierce.

"I'll find a way. There must be something strong enough to smash this thing."

Thrud was looking thoughtful.

"There might be," she said. "But it'll only work if my dad is distracted. Come with me."

———————————————

Once again, they sneaked through the dark streets of Asgard, but nobody was about. Valhalla was full to bursting as they passed.

"That's good," Thrud said. "Hopefully, my dad will be in there, celebrating hard. It sounds like they beat the Frost Giants again."

"What's the plan?" Demon asked.

"You'll see," she said, opening a small door at the back of the hall. The noise hit them like a thump in the chest.

"Stay here and keep guard," she said. "And if you see Greedy and Ravenous, play your pipes at them. If they catch me, they'll ruin everything."

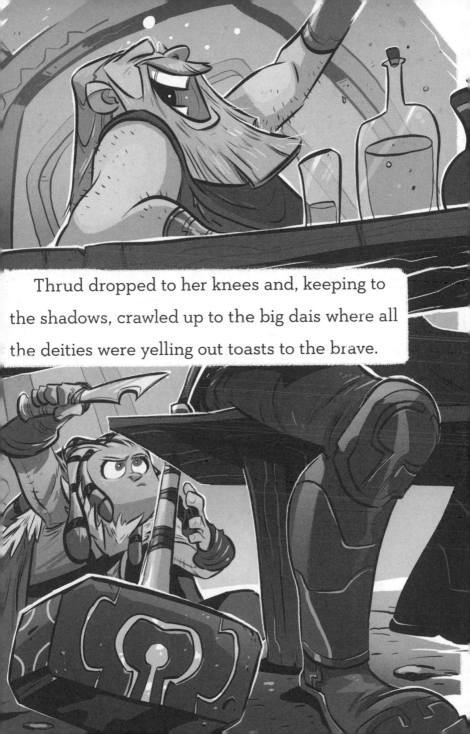

Thrud dropped to her knees and, keeping to the shadows, crawled up to the big dais where all the deities were yelling out toasts to the brave.

Demon bit back a squeak as he saw her draw her dagger and cut Thor's hammer, Mjolnir, off his belt, lowering it silently to the ground. Her arms strained and her face turned beet red at the effort. Then she bent and whispered some words over it, and right away she picked it up as if it were as light as air, and scurried back to where Demon was waiting.

"No sign of the wolves," he said.

"Good. Now let's hurry. Dad will miss this before long, and I'll be in terrible trouble if I don't put it back." She looked at him sideways. "I'm not really supposed to be able to lift it, but I haven't been around Dad all this time without learning a thing or two!"

Thrud said Mjolnir would break the mortar, so Demon cleared a patch on a clean bit of the stable floor and put the ice diamond on it.

"On your mark! Get set! Go!" said Thrud, lifting

the huge hammer above her head. And then she dropped it. BANG! Right on top of the jewel. With a little sigh, the ice diamond dissolved into sparkly red dust.

"There!" said Thrud, delighted with herself. "I knew it would work. Get to work, Demon! I need to take this back to Dad."

Moving faster than the griffin after a meaty bone, Demon scraped the dust into the mortar and added the contents of the spit bottle. As he mixed the ingredients together, they began to glow with an incandescent yellow light. Quickly, he picked up the mortar.

"Open wide," he said to Goldbristle, and tipped the whole lot into the boar's gaping mouth. The effect was immediate. Demon flung his arm over his eyes to keep from being blinded by the brightness as Goldbristle leaped up and did a little capering dance around the stable. Then Goldbristle burst

through the
doors, ran outside,
and galloped up into
the sky, grunting with joy.
Suddenly, light fell
over Asgard, and if
Demon had thought it was beautiful
before, now every snow crystal and icicle
spear shone with a multitude of rainbows,

making the whole place sparkle like not just one, but a million huge diamonds.

Cheers erupted within Valhalla, and all the gods, goddesses, shield-maidens, and warriors poured out into the streets. With a flash, Demon saw Demeter's big greenhouse melt into nothing, revealing rows and rows of plants, flowers, and trees, in a riot of green and color, curling up toward Goldbristle's light.

Frey reached Demon first and threw him into the air, then grabbed him and gave him a god hug that smelled like ripe apples and the sharpness of snow.

"Three cheers for Pandemonius," he shouted. The cry was taken up by everyone there. Then, amid the rejoicing, Odin appeared, with Greedy and Ravenous slinking at his heels, and his ravens, as usual, perched on his shoulders.

Demon fell to his knees, but Odin raised him up at once.

"Well, young healer," the ruler of Asgard boomed. "My ravens say you have a tale to tell us. Come! Let us eat and drink while we hear it, young hero." He made Demon stand on the dais before them all, and between munches of a delicious kind of pastry with apples, raisins, cinnamon, and sparkly white sugar, Demon told them all that had happened.

"But I couldn't have done any of it without Thrud and Ratatosk," he finished, turning to Odin. "They're the real heroes, and . . ." He took a deep breath. "And Thrud really deserves to be a shield-maiden, because she's very brave, and . . . and she fought off the lake serpents and everything."

Odin looked at him with his one eye.

"It appears so," he said. "But before anything else, Loki must be found and dealt with. This is all his fault."

He beckoned to Thor. "Put him in Asgard's

deepest dungeon," he growled. "And this time he shall not escape!"

Thor nodded, fingering Mjolnir, now safely restored to his belt. "It will be my pleasure, All-Father," he said.

Demon sat blushing through many toasts. The gods and goddesses of Asgard certainly knew how to party—and even Demeter was joining in with the praising. Then, just as Thor slipped back into his seat with a nod at Odin, the one-eyed god thumped the table for silence.

"A great deed has been done today," he boomed, "one that songs will be sung about forever in this hall. Stand forth, Ratatosk the squirrel, Thrud Thorsdaughter, and Pandemonius, Stable Master of Olympus."

"Ooh!" said Ratatosk, leaping down from the rafters to land in front of Odin. "Has Ratatosk been clever? Does he get a prize?" Everyone laughed.

"He does, indeed," said Odin, producing a gigantic brown nut out of nowhere. "May you never be hungry again, for this nut cannot be lost, and

will always renew itself." With a squeak of delight, Ratatosk seized the nut and bounced off Ravenous and Greedy's heads, before leaping up into the rafters. The wolves snarled after him.

"Can't catch me, sillies," the squirrel chittered, before disappearing out the window.

"Thrud Thorsdaughter," said Odin. "You have shown bravery and initiative of the highest order. I hereby grant you the status of shield-maiden of Asgard, and give you this." He handed her a hammer, similar to Thor's but about half the size. "Meet Mjolnirina." Thrud blushed scarlet as she mumbled her thanks and went off to sit with the other shield-maidens.

"Now, Pandemonius, son of Pan. What are we to do with you?"

Demon looked at him. "I don't need anything, really, Your Serene Snowiness," he said. "I'm just glad Goldbristle is better."

"But you shall have it, anyway," Odin said. Out of the air, he drew a beautiful medallion with an ash tree embossed on it in diamonds, and a small horn banded with gold and studded with jewels in all the seven colors of the rainbow. "I hereby award you the Order of Yggdrasil, and the freedom of Asgard. You are welcome here, always. I also give you this horn, which is called Far Caller. If you are ever in direst need, blow it, and the warriors of Asgard will come to your aid."

Demon gulped. It was a magnificent gift. "Th-thank you, Your Incredible Iciness," he said, bowing low, just as two black-and-silver heads peered around Odin's cloak.

"Can't we bite you just a little bit now?" Ravenous growled.

"You do look *very* tasty," whined Greedy.

Demon laughed. "Maybe next time, boys," he said, throwing them each a pastry.

GLOSSARY

PRONUNCIATION GUIDE

THE GREEK GODS

Ares (AIR-eez): God of war. Loves any excuse to pick a fight.

Chiron (KY-ron): God of the centaurs. Known for his wisdom and healing abilities.

Demeter (duh-MEE-ter): Goddess of plants and the harvest. The original green thumb.

Dionysus (DY-uh-NY-suss): God of wine. Turns even sensible gods into silly goons.

Hades (HAY-deez): Zeus's brother, the gloomy, fearsome ruler of the Underworld.

Helios (HEE-lee-us): The bright, shiny, and blinding Titan god of the sun.

Hephaestus (hih-FESS-tuss): God of blacksmithing, metalworking, fire, volcanoes, and most things awesome.

Hera (HEER-a): Zeus's scary wife. Drives a chariot pulled by screechy peacocks.

Hestia (HESS-tee-ah): Goddess of the hearth and home. Bakes the most heavenly treats.

Pan (PAN): God of shepherds and flocks. Frequently found wandering grassy hillsides, playing his pipes.

Poseidon (puh-SY-dun): God of the sea and controller of natural and supernatural events.

Zeus (ZOOSS): King of the gods. Fond of smiting people with lightning bolts.

THE NORSE GODS

Frey (FRAY): Shiny, happy god of peace, growth, and sunshine. Twin brother of Freya.

Freya (FRAY-uh): Goddess of love and beauty. Twin sister of Frey.

Heimdall (HAME-doll): Guardian and herald of Asgard. Has a really loud horn.

Idunn (ih-DOON): Goddess who grows golden apples that make you live forever.

Loki (LOW-kee): The sneaky, shape-shifting trickster god of Asgard.

Odin (OH-dinn): The All-Father and ruler of Asgard.

Thor (THOR): Mighty god of thunder who has a giant hammer called Mjolnir (MYAWL-neer).

Thrud (THROOD): Thor's daughter. Well on her way to becoming a Valkyrie.

Tyr (TEER): War god who got his hand bitten off by Fenrir.

OTHER MYTHICAL BEINGS

Amaltheia (ah-mul-THEE-uh): An actual goat who raised Zeus as if he were her own.

Cherubs (CHAIR-ubs): Small flying babies. Mostly cute.

Dryads (DRY-ads): Tree nymphs. Can literally sing trees to life.

Heracles (HAIR-a-kleez): The half-god "hero" who just loooves killing magical beasts.

Hygeia (hy-GEE-uh): Famous for her excellent health and cleanliness . . . or should I say hygiene?

Morpheus (MOR-fee-us): The spirit of dreams. Brings wonderful (or terrible) visions to the sleeping.

Nymphs (NIMFS): Giggly, girly, dancing nature spirits.

Orpheus (OR-fee-us): A musician, a poet, and a real charmer.

Peleus (PEE-lee-us): A hero and the prince of the ant-men. Relies a little too much on his magical sword.

Valkyries (VAL-kuh-reez): The shield-maidens who bring fallen heroes to Valhalla.

PLACES

Asgard (ASS-gard): The chilly Northern home of the Norse gods.

Mount Pelion (PEEL-ee-un): A mountain on the Aegean Sea where Chiron the centaur lives.

Svartalfheim (SVART-alf-hame): Creepy underground home of the dark elves.

Valhalla (vall-HALL-uh): Official party hall for the heroes and Valkyries.

Yggdrasil (IGG-druh-sill): A giant ash tree that keeps the worlds together.

BEASTS

Centaur (SEN-tor): Half man, half horse, and lucky enough to get the best parts of both.

Cerberus (SUR-ber-uss): Three-headed guard dog whose only weaknesses are sunshine and happiness.

Colchian Dragon (KOL-kee-un): Ares's guard dragon. Has magical teeth and *supposedly* never sleeps.

Cretan Bull (KREE-tun): A furious, fire-breathing bull. Don't stand too close.

Fafnir (FAVE-neer): A fearsome cursed dragon who guards a stash of gems and gold.

Fenrir (FEN-reer): Mad wolf who has it out for Odin.

Griffin (GRIH-fin): Couldn't decide if it was better to be a lion or an eagle, so decided to be both.

Gullinbursti (GOO-lin-burst-ee): Also known as Goldbristle, he's a glowing golden boar and friend of Frey.

Hydra (HY-druh): Nine-headed water serpent. Hera somehow finds this lovable.

Khalkotauroi (KALL-koh-tor-OY): Khalko and Kafto, Hephaestus's fire-breathing, half-automaton bronze bulls.

Pegasus (PEG-uh-sus): The mightiest winged horse of all.

Phoenix (FEE-nix): Wondrous bird with a burning desire to be reborn every hundred years.

Ratatosk (RAH-tah-tosk): A red messenger squirrel who runs around in the tree Yggdrasil.

ABOUT THE AUTHOR

Lucy Coats studied English and ancient history at Edinburgh University, then worked in children's publishing, and now writes full-time. She is a gifted children's poet and writes for all ages from two to teenage. She is widely respected for her lively retellings of myths. Her twelve-book series Greek Beasts and Heroes was published by Orion in the UK. Beasts of Olympus is her first US chapter-book series. Lucy's website is www.lucycoats.com. You can also follow her on Twitter @lucycoats.

ABOUT THE ILLUSTRATOR

As a kid, **Brett Bean** made stuff up to get out of trouble. As an adult, Brett makes stuff up to make people happy. Brett creates art for film, TV, games, books, and toys. He works on his tan and artwork in California with his wife, Julie Anne, and son, Finnegan Hobbes. He hopes to leave the world a little bit better for having him. You can find more about Brett and his artwork at www.drawntoitstudios.com.